NO MONEY?
NO PROBLEM!

by Lori Haskins
illustrated by John Nez

The Kane
New York

Library of Congress Cataloging-in-Publication Data

Haskins, Lori.
  No money? No problem! / by Lori Haskins ; illustrated by John Nez.
      p. cm. — (Social Studies connects)
  "Economics - grades: K–2."
  Summary: Amy, desperate to get her hands on the latest video game, learns how people acquired things before money existed, and decides to take a lesson from history.
  ISBN 1-57565-141-6 (pbk. : alk. paper)
  [1. Barter—Fiction.] I. Nez, John A., ill. II. Title. III. Series.
  PZ7.H27645No 2004
  [Fic]—dc22
                                                    2003024179

10 9 8 7 6 5 4 3 2 1

First published in the United States of America in 2004 by The Kane Press.
Printed in Hong Kong.

Social Studies Connects is a trademark of The Kane Press.

Book Design/Art Direction: Edward Miller

www.kanepress.com

Amy's eyes were glued to the store window.
There it was—*Super Cowboy Dinosaurs from Space*,
the greatest video game ever. She sighed.

There was no use dreaming about it. All the
stores were sold out. Even if they weren't, she
could never afford it.

"What's up, Amy?" asked Matt.

"Nothing," she said. But she was still staring at the store window.

"You know, I have an extra copy of that game," Matt said. "Both my grandmas gave it to me for my birthday."

"ARE YOU *SERIOUS*?" shouted Amy.

"Er—yeah," said Matt. "I was going to return one. But if you want, I can sell it to you instead. I'll even give you a good price."

"Great!" Amy said.

Amy emptied her piggy bank the minute she got home. "Fifty, fifty-one, fifty-two," she counted.

"Wow! You have fifty-two dollars?" said her brother, Ben, leaning on his crutches.

"Fifty-two *cents*," moaned Amy. "I'll never save enough for *Super Cowboy Dinosaurs from Space*."

"Bummer," Ben said. "Hey, Mom says to come downstairs. She wants us to watch the Brainiac show."

Amy rolled her eyes. "More educational TV," she muttered. But she followed Ben downstairs.

"Brainiac wouldn't be so bad if it weren't for the host," thought Amy. Mr. Bob had the world's dullest voice. It always put her to sleep.

Amy's eyelids started to droop.

"Up next: *No Money? No Problem!*" said Mr. Bob.
Amy's eyes flew open.
"What did people do before they used money?"
Mr. Bob went on. "Find out now, on Brainiac!"
"Turn it up!" Amy yelled.

Mr. Bob's voice boomed out of the TV. "Before money was popular, people all over the world used to barter, or trade, to get what they needed."

A picture flashed on the screen.

"A baker might trade a sack of flour for a pair of boots," Mr. Bob said.

Trade you?

Deal!

Sometimes people bartered goods, which were things they had.

"A carpenter might fix a wagon in exchange for a nice plump pig," he continued. "The barter system wasn't perfect. But it worked well enough to last thousands of years!"

"That's it!" said Amy. "I'll *barter* with Matt for the game!"

Sometimes people bartered services, which were things they did.

I'll pull out your bad tooth.

I'll shoe your horse!

Amy raced up to her room. What could she trade? She found an old dictionary, an even older globe, and a slightly used Ping-Pong paddle. She started shoving things in her backpack.

Then she biked over to Matt's house.

Let's swap?

Okay!

You may not know it, but you've probably bartered. Have you ever traded your cupcake for someone's cookies at lunch? That's bartering!

"I wouldn't mind trading the game for *something*," Matt said. "Just not this stuff."

Amy was disappointed, but she understood. None of her goods were—well, all that good.

Right then Amy decided what to do. She'd barter her things for better things. And she'd keep on trading until she had something Matt couldn't resist!

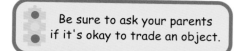

Be sure to ask your parents if it's okay to trade an object.

It didn't take Amy long to get the hang of bartering. The key was finding people who wanted what you had.

"If you cut this globe in half, it would make a nice birdbath," Amy told Mrs. Brown.

"What a great idea!" Mrs. Brown said. "Would you trade it for a Ping-Pong paddle?"

"Deal!" said Amy.

Now Amy had *two* paddles. She traded them with the Crockett twins. They had been talking about setting up a Ping-Pong table in their yard. "I'll even throw in the ball," Amy told them.

The Crockett twins gave Amy a pair of old rollerblades.

Amy went to see Mr. Mendez across the street. He couldn't use the rollerblades, but he wanted the dictionary.

"It's just what I need," he said. "I'll trade you that wind sock for it."

Bartering wasn't always so easy. Some of the stuff was a real pain to carry around.

"Oops! Watch your head!"

There has to be a better way . . .

People had the same problem a long time ago. It was hard to lug around sacks of flour and barrels of salt. That's one reason people changed from bartering to using money.

And sometimes Amy wound up with something nobody wanted.

"Paper clips? Paper clips, anyone?"

People in different places used different things as money—salt, dried fish, and even chocolate! Money could be anything that everybody agreed was valuable.

But sometimes she wound up with something
EVERYBODY wanted!

"Get this giant box of bubble gum!" Amy cried.
"Blow bubbles all summer long!"

Almost everybody agreed that gold was
valuable. So people started using gold coins
as money. But the coins
were very heavy to carry
around. Then the Chinese
invented paper money.
It was a lot lighter!

Amy had made some smart trades. But she still wasn't sure her stuff would knock Matt's socks off. "What do you think?" she asked Ben.

Ben frowned. "You need something really awesome. Hold on! I've got it!"

Ben limped away.

He was back in two minutes.

"Your Mega Radical Turbo Action Skateboard?" gasped Amy. "Really?"

"I broke my ankle showing off on this thing!" Ben said. "Trust me—I'm never using it again."

"So what should I trade you for it?" asked Amy. "My remote control car?"

"Well, that—plus something else," said Ben. "Remember on the Brainiac show, how they said that sometimes instead of trading stuff they *had*, people traded stuff they *did*? Well, I have a little chore for you."

"I can't believe I'm doing this," muttered Amy, scratching Ben's stinky foot.

But it was worth it. The Turbo Action Skateboard was sure to impress Matt. Before the day was over, *Super Cowboy Dinosaurs from Space* would be hers!

"COOL!" yelled Matt as soon as he spotted the skateboard. He handed Amy the video game right away.

"Just be careful," she warned. "You know what happened to Ben!"

"Okay," Matt promised.

Amy stared at the box in her hand. Wow!

Now she didn't have to worry about bartering anymore. She could play *Super Cowboy Dinosaurs* for the rest of the summer!

Bye-bye, money?

Almost every country in the world uses money. People think that some day in the future credit cards will replace coins and paper money.

The game was great—just as great as Amy had thought it would be. She played it over and over.

Something was bugging her, though. Could it be that she missed bartering?

All that wheeling and dealing *was* kind of fun!
But what would be the point now? She already
had what she wanted.

Before she knew it, Amy found herself in front of
the toy store. There was a new sign in the window.
"Coming Soon—*Super Cowboy Dinosaurs from
Space* **2**! Order Your Copy Now!"

She could hardly believe it.

"Hey, Amy," called Matt. "You'll never guess what both my grandmas ordered for me."

Amy grinned. "I bet I can! And I bet I'll find something to trade you for it."

"Let's make a deal! What have you got to trade, folks? Step right up!" Amy was back in business!

Wow! Just what I always wanted.

People still barter today. Remember, one person's throwaway is another person's treasure!

I can predict!

MAKING CONNECTIONS

When you *predict*, you guess what is likely to happen.

Predicting is a very important part of bartering. You have to predict who will want what! You also have to find people who want what you have to trade—and that's not easy.

Look Back

On page 15 how did Amy predict that the Crockett twins might want her Ping-Pong paddle?

Look at page 16. What was Mr. Mendez doing when Amy arrived? Could Amy have predicted that he would want a dictionary? How?

Try This!

Pretend Matt has something you want. These are the things you have to trade. Can you predict what Matt might like?

CAT CARE

Things You Have to Trade

Toothpaste

Talk with some friends. Do they have things they'd like to trade with you?